SUPER DC HEROES

SUPERMAN

THE SHRINKING CITY

WRITTEN BY
MICHAEL DAHL

ILLUSTRATED BY
GREGG SCHIGIEL AND
LEE LOUGHRIDGE

SUPERMAN CREATED BY
JERRY SIEGEL AND
JOE SHUSTER

STONE ARCH BOOKS
MINNEAPOLIS   SAN DIEGO

Published by Stone Arch Books in 2010
151 Good Counsel Drive, P.O. Box 669
Mankato, Minnesota 56002
www.stonearchbooks.com

Library of Congress Cataloging-in-Publication Data

Dahl, Michael.
  The shrinking city / by Michael Dahl ; illustrated by Gregg Schigiel.
    p. cm. -- (DC super heroes. Superman)
  ISBN 978-1-4342-1569-7 (lib. bdg.) -- ISBN 978-1-4342-1735-6 (pbk.)
  [1. Superheroes--Fiction.] I. Schigiel, Gregg, ill. II. Title.
  PZ7.D15134Sh 2010
  [Fic]--dc22
                                        2009008738

Summary: Thirty years ago, Brainiac shrank the city of Kandor and sealed it
inside an unbreakable glass container. The evil supercomputer is still exploring
the universe, collecting cities from hundreds of planets. Superman must stop
Brainiac from bottling up Metropolis, and then save Kandor — the last
remnant of his home planet.

Art Director: Bob Lentz
Designer: Bob Lentz

Printed in the United States of America

TABLE OF CONTENTS

CHAPTER 1

THE STOLEN CITY

Thirty years ago, in a distant galaxy, the planet Krypton was rocked by powerful earthquakes. Cities across the entire planet shook and swayed. In the gleaming city of Kandor, buildings trembled. People screamed. Fire and smoke poured through cracks in the streets.

Hax-Ur and Zan, two men from Kandor, jumped into a flyer pod. Their mission was to find Krypton's most famous scientist, Jor-El. "If anyone can explain these earthquakes," said Zan, "Jor-El can."

Jor-El, his scientist wife, Lara, and their infant son Kal-El lived in Kryptonopolis, the capital city of Krypton. Hax-Ur typed the city's location into the flyer's control panel. "If Jor-El cannot help us, then Kandor is doomed," he said.

CRASH! Glass from broken windows shattered in the streets. **BOOM!** Several buildings burst into flames.

"There's no time to lose," said Zan. He waved his hand over the control panel. The flyer shot forward. It zoomed past the trembling buildings. It flew through falling walls and thick smoke. Soon it reached the city limits.

"According to the flyer's computer, we will reach Kryptonopolis in fifteen minutes," said Hax-Ur.

SMASH! The flyer crashed into an invisible barrier. The metal ripped and crunched. Luckily, the ship's safety system had surrounded the young men in floating air bubbles. But the flyer was smashed beyond repair. Its hull lay on the ground, twisted and smoking.

"What — what happened?" cried Zan.

Hax-Ur stepped out of his safety bubble. He walked past the flyer and put his hand into the air. "There's a barrier here," he said. "An invisible force field."

"Then we're trapped," said Zan. His eyes were wide with fear. "We won't be able to reach Jor-El."

"We can't leave Kandor at all," said Hax-Ur. "But who put this wall around the city? And why?"

"Hax-Ur," said his friend. "Your skin is turning blue!"

Both men's complexions had changed color.

The friends looked up. A loud hum vibrated through the air.

"What's that?" said Hax-Ur.

He pointed to a strange ship floating high above Kandor. A weird blue light was blazing from the bottom of the ship. It shed its glow over the entire city.

The young men watched as powerful cannons appeared from the sides of the strange ship. They aimed toward the ground.

"Look out!" yelled Zan.

ZZRRRRTT! White-hot laser beams shot from the mouths of the cannons. The beams blasted the ground on the other side of the invisible wall. Hax-Ur and Zan watched, dazed, as the lasers dug a deep trench in the ground.

"They're digging through solid rock!" said Zan, gasping.

In only a few minutes, the operation was complete. The lasers stopped. The trench now circled Kandor. Suddenly, a rumbling sound filled the air. The ground began to shake, but it was not an earthquake.

WHAM! Hax-Ur and Zan were hurled off their feet. The entire city of Kandor seemed to sway. The young men did not know it, but their whole city was being lifted into the air by an unseen force.

The strange ship was pulling Kandor away from the planet Krypton. The men did not know that the invisible barrier was actually a wall of unbreakable glass. It trapped Kandor's air inside, letting its people breathe. The entire city of Kandor was imprisoned.

They did not know that the city was shrinking. Soon it would be stuck inside its bottle forever. It would sit among a collection of other cities from across the galaxy. The stolen cities belonged to the owner of the strange ship. And now that Kandor was his new prize, he steered away from the dying planet. Krypton would soon explode, but Kandor would survive.

For now.

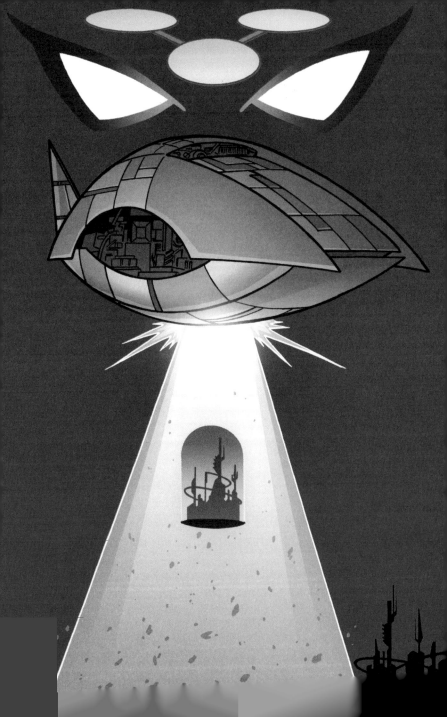

CHAPTER 2

VISITOR FROM SPACE

Thirty years later, two astronomers at the Metropolis Observatory made an incredible discovery.

"It's coming straight toward the Earth!" cried the older astronomer. "But it doesn't look like a regular meteor."

His young partner stared into the eyepiece of a gigantic telescope. Then she shook her head. "You're right, it's not a meteor," she said. "It looks like a ship to me."

"Ship?" said the man. He took another look through the eyepiece and frowned. "I think we had better call Superman."

For weeks, other astronomers and scientists around the world had been tracking the path of the strange object. Experts thought it was a comet heading toward the sun. Others thought it was a meteor. But now, the object was close enough to be seen more clearly.

"I've never seen anything move so fast," said the young woman.

Her partner picked up the phone. "Get me the *Daily Planet*," he said to the operator. "This is an emergency!"

In the offices of the *Daily Planet*, the major newspaper of Metropolis, a phone rang.

Jimmy Olsen, cub reporter and photographer, quickly picked up the phone. "Olsen here," he said. As he listened to the caller, a sudden look of amazement swept over his face.

"Jimmy, what's wrong?" asked Lois Lane. She sat at a nearby desk. Lane was one of the *Planet*'s top reporters. She was also Jimmy's friend.

Jimmy nodded his head as he continued to listen. "Yes, sir," said Jimmy. "I'll do it right away."

CLICK! He hung up the phone's receiver and stared at Lois.

"You know that meteor the scientists have been watching for the past month?" he asked.

Lois nodded. "Of course," she said.

Lois continued, "I have an interview with the astronomers at Metropolis Observatory later this afternoon."

"Well, you can save yourself the trip, Miss Lane," said Jimmy. "They just called and said they want me to contact Superman. That's no meteor out there!"

"What are you talking about, Jimmy?" Lois asked.

"It's a spaceship," he said. "And it could reach Earth in just a few hours!"

Jimmy ran over to a window. Then he pressed a button on his wristwatch and held it next to the glass. **BEEP! BEEP!**

The button sent out a signal that only one person could hear — Superman. And whenever Superman heard it, he knew it meant just one thing. Jimmy needed help.

Lois glanced around the office. Then she shrugged and folded her arms. "It figures that Clark wouldn't be here," she said. "The whole world is going to be visited by aliens, and Clark Kent is probably spilling something on his tie at lunch somewhere."

Lois and Jimmy didn't realize that Clark Kent, their fellow reporter, was merely the disguise of Superman himself. He was the world's most powerful super hero.

WHOOOOSH!

Startled, Jimmy stepped back from the window. A huge grin stretched across his face. "There he goes," said Jimmy. "Superman must have known about the spaceship even before we got the call."

Superman waved at Jimmy and Lois as he soared past the Daily Planet office.

The hero flew above the building. He zoomed past the city's tallest skyscrapers.

Minutes before Jimmy's signal-watch had alerted him, Superman had heard an unusual sound, and the hero's super-hearing traced it to the strange object in space.

Superman raced far above the stratosphere. Suddenly, he saw a spaceship fly into view.

"That ship is faster than anything I've seen before," Superman said to himself. "I just hope it comes here in peace."

Superman's hope was quickly dashed. From the sides of the ship, twin powerful cannons appeared. They aimed toward the flying man. White-hot laser beams shot from the cannons. ZZAPPPPPPP!

CHAPTER 3

ATTACK ON METROPOLIS

"Ughhh!" Superman groaned. The beams struck him right in his chest.

The mighty hero was hurled backward several miles, still floating high above the surface of Earth.

Superman righted himself and raced back toward the strange ship. He saw a porthole opening in the ship's hull. Thick black smoke shot from the porthole.

An evil-looking missile was heading straight toward the Man of Steel.

Superman zigged and zagged. He swooped through vast banks of clouds. The missile was still close behind him. It followed his every move.

He was not afraid of being hurt by the weapon. After all, his skin was invulnerable. Nothing could hurt him. Instead, Superman was worried that the missile's explosion might destroy one of Earth's many weather satellites. Or the blast might damage any planes flying in the area.

Superman flew straight up, higher and higher above the planet. The blue sky faded to black. The stars grew brighter. Then, Superman turned to face the oncoming missile. He shut his eyes and braced himself for the attack. **KA-BOOM!** The missile exploded against Superman's body.

Incredible heat blazed against the hero for several seconds. It felt hotter than the sun. Pieces of metal and plastic were flung into space.

The Man of Steel shook his head. The explosion had dazed him. For a few seconds he stayed where he was, soaking up the bright yellow rays of the sun. He could feel himself growing stronger with each second that passed.

Superman had come to Earth thirty years before. He was a visitor from the distant planet Krypton. He had escaped the destruction of his home world when his scientist father sent him to Earth in a tiny rocket. The yellow sun, so different from Krypton's red sun, gave Superman amazing powers. He always used his powers to protect the people of Earth.

Superman looked for the strange ship. It was gone. No, it was heading downward toward the planet. In fact, it was flying straight toward Metropolis!

I can't let that ship get near the city, he thought.

The Man of Steel zoomed down toward the ship. A weird, blue light blazed from beneath its hull. The light seemed to wrap the entire city of Metropolis in its eerie glow.

Once more, lasers fired from the ship's cannons. **BZZT!** The powerful beams began to dig a trench around Metropolis. Then a wall of glass rose upward, covering the city like a dome.

What's going on? the super hero wondered.

To his horror, Superman saw the city of Metropolis being lifted from the ground. Then, it floated up to the strange ship. It soared faster and faster past the clouds.

"I can't risk breaking through that glass barrier," said Superman. "It might destroy the city." He thought of his friends. Jimmy and Lois were both trapped by this strange invader from space.

Superman changed his direction. Now he sped toward the spaceship itself. He lowered his head, clenched his fists, and increased his speed. The Man of Steel broke through the ship's hull. CRUNCH!

In front of him, he saw a strange, metal figure standing by a blinking control panel. The figure, a supercomputer shaped like a man, turned toward him. His metal head and glowing eyes towered above Superman.

CHAPTER 4

BRAINIAC

"Finally," said the machine. "I have waited a long time to meet the son of Jor-El."

"Jor-El? How do you know that name?" asked Superman.

The figure's eyes glowed brighter. "I am Braniac," he said. "I'm from Krypton, like you. I know all about you, Kal-El." The figure turned and pushed a few buttons on his control panel. "But I did not know how strong you have become."

"You survived my laser blast as well as my armed missile without so much as a scratch!" Brainiac added.

Superman took a step forward. "Return the city of Metropolis to its former location," he said.

Brainiac shook his head. "You are as stubborn as your father," he said.

"How did you know my father?" asked Superman.

"We served together on the science council of Krypton," said Brainiac. "The scientists had created me to be their smartest, fastest computer. I was built to give them the best advice. But your father, Jor-El, was brilliant. And they started listening to his warnings instead of me."

"Warnings?" asked Superman.

"He told them that Krypton would explode," replied Brainiac. "The planet was doomed."

"They would have listened to his advice too," added Brainiac. "But I convinced them that your father was wrong."

Superman had heard enough. He lunged toward the metallic figure.

SLAM! He crashed into an invisible barrier. Brainiac had surrounded himself with a protective force field. The Man of Steel was hurled backward onto the floor.

"You cannot defeat my superior mind," said Brainiac. "Neither could the council. Besides, why did those people need to exist? They all would have died one day, anyway. Krypton's knowledge was in my computer. The planet was no longer needed."

"You killed them by lying to them," said Superman. "You destroyed Krypton."

"Earthquakes destroyed Krypton," said Brainiac. The supercomputer walked past Superman. He stood next to a round glass door. "Come with me, Kal-El," he said. "I will show you what survives from Krypton. Besides yourself, that is."

The supercomputer led Superman down a long hall. Soon, they stood in a large room filled with tall bottles. Inside each bottle rested a miniature city. Above each bottle hung a glowing orb, green or blue or yellow or red.

"You make models?" asked a puzzled Superman.

"Not quite," the supercomputer responded, smiling.

"These are real cities," explained Brainiac. "I have been collecting them for the past thirty Earth years. I have gathered them from galaxies all the way from Krypton to your solar system here."

"You mean you stole them," said Superman.

He bent down and stared through the glass of a nearby bottle. He could see small flying ships buzzing about the buildings. Tiny creatures filled the streets. There were even miniature clouds floating near the top of the bottle.

"And the orbs are their suns?" asked the super hero.

"Not their real suns, of course," said Brainiac. "But real enough to give the cities the same light as their original suns."

"This is what you plan to do to Metropolis, isn't it?" said Superman.

"It's already happening," said Brainiac. "The Earth city is undergoing the shrinking process. Soon it will join my collection. But aren't you going to ask me about that bottle over there, Kal-El?"

Brainiac waved to a bottle that stood in a far corner. It rested on a pedestal larger and more ornate than the others. It clearly held a special place among this strange collection. And above its domed glass blazed an orb of red light.

"Yes," said Brainiac. "That is from Krypton. It is the city of Kandor. Perfectly preserved within its unbreakable glass. Beautiful, isn't it?"

"You can't do this," said Superman.

"I already have," said Brainiac. "And that's not all that I took from Krypton. There is this, as well!"

The metal figure opened a nearby cabinet and pulled out a glowing green rock. He held it out toward Superman in one of his metal hands. Instantly, Superman felt weak, as if someone had punched him in the stomach.

"Kryptonite!" he gasped.

"Exactly! A piece of your home planet," said Brainiac.

When Krypton exploded, it burst into a billion pieces. Once the pieces were far from the red sun, they became radioactive. They were deadly to anyone from Krypton.

Superman hunched over in agony. He had never felt such pain before.

"Do you feel your life draining away?" asked Brainiac. "It will all be over soon."

FLASH! A light on the wall began to blink rapidly.

"Ahh," said Brainiac. "The city of Metropolis is now completely shrunk. I'm sorry you won't be around to see it, Superman. Metropolis will make a fine addition to my collection. Perhaps I will put it next to Kandor. The twin cities of Superman. The two planets that saw his birth . . . and his death!"

Superman fell to his knees. His last thoughts were of Metropolis. He would never see Lois or Jimmy again. They would be shrunk to microscopic size within the tiny city. They would be trapped there forever.

CHAPTER 5

THE RED SUN

"I would shrink you too," said Brainiac. "But I'm afraid you'd still have your superpowers. You'd find some way to escape from the bottle. I can't risk you destroying my beautiful collection."

Superman lifted his head, although it was painful to move. "Krypton," he whispered. "Let me see Krypton."

The lights in Brainiac's metal head glowed and blinked. "Yes," said the supercomputer. "Go and behold the shrunken city of Kandor."

"The Last Son of Krypton gazing at the last city of Krypton. Quite fitting. If I had emotions, I might almost think it was touching," Brainiac said.

Slowly, painfully, Superman crawled to the bottle that held the city of Kandor.

Brainiac followed closely behind him. He still clutched the deadly piece of kryptonite in his hand.

After what seemed like hours to Superman, he finally reached the bottled city. His hand gently touched the glass. His fingertips brushed against it. He squinted and stared at the tiny city. "Krypton," he whispered again. He watched as tiny clouds within the bottle shaded parts of Kandor from the blaze of its miniature sun.

Its *red* sun.

Closer and closer, Superman huddled next to the bottle. He reached around it and held it tightly in his arms. The world that was his first home, the world of his dead father and mother, now rested within his grasp. His eyes stared into the small, blazing red orb.

Its bright rays cast a reddish glow over the entire bottle. Superman's skin turned red in the light.

"I must leave you now," said Brainiac. He set the kryptonite on the floor. "I have to take care of my new prize."

Brainiac turned to leave. Just then, a sudden light filled the room. The supercomputer felt a strong breeze blow between the bottles.

"What?!" he screamed.

Superman had opened a nearby hatch in the ship's hull and thrown himself out. Faster and faster he plummeted toward the Earth. He shot like a comet past layers of clouds. The yellow rays of the sun reflected off his uniform.

"But how?" said Brainiac. "He was too weak. He would never have been able to open that hatch. He had no strength!"

The ship began to shiver and sway. "It can't be," said Brainiac.

Superman, his strength restored, had returned to the supercomputer's ship. He was pushing it closer to Earth — back toward Earth's atmosphere.

Just then, Brainiac's supercomputer brain told him the truth.

"The red sun!" he said. "Of course! Beneath the red rays of the duplicate sun of Krypton, Superman no longer had his superpowers. He was like a regular Kryptonian. So he was no longer affected by the original piece of his planet. The chunk of kryptonite was like a normal rock to him!"

SHREEE-EEE-EEECH! Superman ripped a hole in the side of the ship. Using his super-breath, he blew the chunk of kryptonite out of the ship. It flew far into space, beyond the orbit of the Moon.

Then he quickly flew to Brainiac's control panel. His super-brain figured out how to reverse the beam that was shrinking Metropolis. Outside the ship, Superman swiftly soared to a spot beneath the growing city.

The city had been floating up to Brainiac's ship, but now that it was returning to its original size, it had begun to fall back toward Earth.

Superman supported the entire city of Metropolis with his bare hand. He flew toward Earth, carefully balancing his precious cargo. Down and down, he dropped.

Inside the Daily Planet Building, Jimmy Olsen pointed out the window. "Look, Miss Lane!" he said. "Now the clouds are moving up again."

"What's going on?" asked Lois. She was holding onto her desk to keep from falling over. For the past half hour, the entire city had been rocking and swaying. It felt like they were caught in a small earthquake.

"And what happened to that weird ship?" Lois asked. "The one that everyone thought was a meteor?"

Jimmy shook his head. "I don't know," he said. "I can't see it now."

"Well, whatever is going on," said Lois. "I'm sure Superman is fighting to keep us all safe."

Superman's feet finally touched down on Earth. His boots dug into the solid rock as he sank into the ground and placed Metropolis smoothly into its original position. Then, from below the city, he burrowed at super-speed. He emerged several miles away.

"I'll come back later to repair the tunnel," he told himself. "But first things first . . . "

Like a rocket exploding from the dirt, he rushed back toward Brainiac's ship.

I can do the same thing to Kandor, thought the Man of Steel. *I'll reverse the shrinking process.*

But as he neared the ship, he saw a small pod escape through a hatch in the back of the hull. Brainiac was fleeing!

A voice vibrated through the air.

"You may have saved Metropolis," said Brainiac through a speaker on his pod. "But my ship will self-destruct in a few seconds. You decide, Kal-El. You only have time to stop me or save Kandor. You cannot do both!"

Superman rushed into the ship. He threw his arms around the bottled city.

The ship exploded. Flames engulfed the super hero. After several seconds of intense heat, the ship dissolved around him. But shielded by the Man of Steel, the city was kept safe.

Superman watched Brainiac's pod disappear into space. Then he gazed down at the bottled city in his hands. The last city of Krypton. His father had tried to save the entire planet. At least his son could now save a piece of it.

"Some day I will return you to your original size," he said. "I promise."

Then, holding the city gently in one arm, Superman flew back toward the surface of his adopted home.

Within Kandor's glass bottle, two middle-aged men were flying above the city in a sleek, silver pod. Suddenly, Zan cried out in surprise.

"Zan, what is it?" asked his longtime friend, Hax-Ur. "What's wrong?"

The other man rubbed his eyes. "I thought I saw something," he said.

"What was it?" asked Hax-Ur.

"Not an *it*," said Zan. "A *person*. I thought I saw a face in the clouds."

"You must have been dreaming," said his friend.

"It was the face of Jor-El," said Zan. "I'm sure it was."

"Jor-El?" Hax-Ur rested a hand on his friend's shoulder.

"Well, even if it was a dream, it was a good dream," Hax-Ur said. "Perhaps someday Jor-El will finally come and rescue us. He'll save us from this terrible prison of glass."

"Yes, perhaps," said Zan. "They say that Jor-El is a good man. If anyone can save us, he can."

"Never give up hope," said Hax-Ur.

"No," said Zan. " I never will."

DAILY PLANET

WHO IS BRAINIAC?

Of all the super-villains that Superman has faced, Brainiac is one of the most sinister. His cold and calculating mind is as vast as the universe itself. He has led countless civilizations to extinction in order to harvest their technologies — including Superman's home planet, Krypton. Brainiac uses his huge stores of stolen knowledge to outsmart and overcome anyone who stands in his way. Only Superman himself is capable of matching wits with the walking, talking supercomputer.

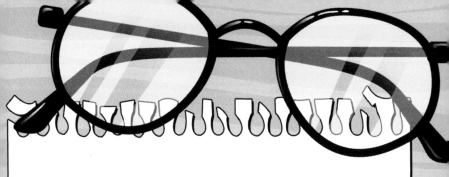

- Brainiac has invented many gadgets. His force-field belt protects him from attackers by surrounding him with a protective shield of energy. He has even created a weapon that sprays a mist of kryptonite!

- Brainiac has a device that is capable of controlling space and time. He also has a weapon that can shrink entire worlds, so he can add them to his collection.

- No matter how many times Brainiac's body is destroyed, he always finds a way to save his brain. This ability allows Brainiac to rise again whenever he finds a suitable body. Once, he even merged with the city of Metropolis itself!

- In just a few hours, Brainiac remade Metropolis into an entirely new city. Many buildings and were changed and given upgrades. The large, metal globe that sat atop the Daily Planet building became a giant, realistic hologram.

BIOGRAPHIES

Michael Dahl is the author of more than 200 books for children and young adults. He has won the AEP Distinguished Achievement Award three times for his non-fiction. His Finnegan Zwake mystery series was shortlisted twice by the Anthony and Agatha awards. He has also written the Library of Doom series and the Dragonblood books. He is a featured speaker at conferences around the country on graphic novels and high-interest books for boys.

Gregg Schigiel is originally from South Florida. He knew he wanted to be a cartoonist when he was 11 years old. He's worked on projects featuring Batman, Spider-Man, SpongeBob SquarePants, and just about everything in between. Schigiel currently lives and works in New York City.

Lee Loughridge has been working in comics for more than 14 years. He currently lives in sunny California in a tent on the beach.

GLOSSARY

barrier (BA-ree-ur)—an object that prevents things from passing through it

braced (BRAYSSD)—if you brace yourself, you prepare for something

comet (KOM-it)—a bright space object with a long tail of light that orbits the sun

emerge (i-MURJ)—to come into the open

fleeing (FLEE-ing)—running away from danger

invulnerable (in-VUHL-nur-uh-buhl)—impossible to be harmed or damaged

meteor (MEE-tee-ur)—an object from space that falls into the Earth's atmosphere

ornate (or-NAYT)—richly decorated or fancy

radioactive (ray-dee-oh-AK-tiv)—if something is radioactive, it emits harmful energy

restored (ri-STORD)—returned to normal

trench (TRENCH)—a long, narrow ditch

vast (VAST)—huge in size

DISCUSSION QUESTIONS

1. Superman chose to save the bottled city of Kandor rather than catch Brainiac and stop him once and for all. Do you think he made the right decision?

2. Brainiac believes that information is what matters most — not life itself. What do you think?

3. Clark Kent's secret identity is Superman. If you were a super hero, would you keep your identity a secret? Why?

WRITING PROMPTS

1. Zan mistakes Superman's face for that of his father, Jor-El, because they look very similar to each other. In what ways are you similar to your family members? In what ways are you different?

2. Pretend that Superman was able to to catch Brainiac *and* save Kandor. Describe the battle that takes place between them.

3. Brainiac likes to shrink cities and add them to his collection. If you had a shrinking ray, what would you use it to collect? Mountains? Buildings? Animals? People? Write about your special collection.

WAIT!!

DON'T CLOSE THE BOOK!

THERE'S MORE!